Tudor Rose

A Timepiece Novel

Anne Perry

To Scuff

First published in 2011 in Great Britain by
Barrington Stoke Ltd
18 Walker Street, Edinburgh, EH3 7LP

www.barringtonstoke.co.uk

ISBN: 978-1-84299-317-0

Printed in China by Leo

23775

Contents

Chapter 1
Detention

Rosie sat down at her desk and tried to make sure it looked like she didn't want to be there. That was always the best thing to do in school. If Stacey and Jade had any idea that Rosie thought their classes weren't totally lame they would make her life hell. If she let on she knew the answer to even one question all her so-called friends would think she was a total swot and turn and stare at her and laugh.

At the front of the class Mr Jones started to talk about Queen Elizabeth the First and the Spanish Armada. Everyone was meant to have read about it at home the night before and Rosie had spent hours trying to read the pages Mr Jones had set them in the history textbook. But Rosie hated reading. The letters on the page seemed to be different every time she looked at them, as if they moved when she blinked.

Mr Jones was short and quite fat around the middle, and his hair stuck out. He looked a bit like a hedgehog. He was alright, though, and Rosie wished she could do better in history so he would smile at her and make one of his famous bad jokes.

"Rosie?" Mr Jones' voice cut across her thoughts.

Rosie stared back at him. "Yes, Mr Jones?"

"How many ships were there in the Armada?" Mr Jones asked.

Rosie knew the answer – it was in the book, and at least numbers were easy to read. Should she say? Better not. Stacey would call her a geek and she hated that.

"I don't know," she said in a quiet voice.

"Oh, come on, Rosie!" Mr Jones replied in a tired voice. "I know you can do better than that. Next thing you'll say you don't even know what the Armada was."

Rosie's face felt hot. She had to say something. "It was Spanish, sir."

Mr Jones shook his head in despair.

Stacey and Jade started to snigger. They were on Rosie's side now.

Then Laura Webb put up her hand. She looked like a big, geeky owl with her round glasses and her smug smile. She knew Mr Jones would ask her for the answer next, and as always, she would know it.

Stacey and Jade had started to laugh at Laura now. She was such a loser. Why did she always draw attention to herself like that?

Mr Jones turned to Laura. "Well, Laura? I suppose you can tell Rosie the answer?"

"The Armada was a fleet of ships, sir," Laura said in a smug voice. "King Philip of Spain sent it to invade England. There were

130 ships in total. 22 ships of war and 108 trading ships."

"Well, Laura," said Mr Jones. "It's nice to see that *someone* did their homework."

"Swot!" Stacey shouted. Everyone laughed. At first Rosie joined in, but then she noticed that Zack Edwards was looking really angry. Rosie liked Zack. He was fun to talk to. He knew lots about books, and music, and he didn't go on about cars and football all the time like other boys. He smelled nice and he would look straight at you when he spoke to you, instead of going red. He was really good-looking, too.

Mr Jones glared at the class. "Settle down, people. That's enough."

Rosie sneaked a look at Laura Webb. Laura had gone all red in the face and Rosie felt a bit bad for her.

When Rosie looked up again Mr Jones caught her eye. "Well, Rosie," he said. "Perhaps you can tell me why King Philip of Spain sent a great fleet of ships to invade England. That's not too hard a question."

Rosie went even redder than Laura Webb. She searched and searched her mind for a sensible answer but she couldn't think of what the book had said. Perhaps she hadn't read that bit – there had been too much text in the book for her to read it all. Luckily Jade saved her.

"Because Spain is on the other side of the sea, sir," Jade said. "They couldn't get across or they'd get their feet wet."

This time everyone laughed – except Mr Jones. His face went bright red and his hair stuck up even more than before. "Right!" he shouted. "If you girls think you're so funny, you can stay behind after school this afternoon. In fact, the whole class can stay here until 5 o'clock, and see how funny you think that is!"

Everyone started to shout at once.

"I can't, sir, I've got to – "

"That's not fair, sir! I didn't laugh!"

"But sir, my dad will kill me!"

"You should have thought of that before," Mr Jones said. He was still very red. "Now you're all staying and that's that."

There were more groans, and no one thought Rosie or Jade were the least bit funny any more. In fact, the looks they gave them made Rosie feel more like some kind of smelly dog mess they had found sticking to their shoes.

She didn't dare look at Zack.

Chapter 2
Home Sweet Home

Rosie felt rotten as she crossed the playground after detention. No one had said anything to her when at last they were allowed to go home but she knew that they were angry with her from the way they looked at her. No one ever said anything to her face when she had pissed them off – they were too scared of her, and of Stacey and Jade.

To tell the truth, Rosie didn't want other kids to be scared of her. Stacey and Jade did, because they hated school. Rosie didn't hate school, but sometimes it was easier to let on she did. The thing was that classes like history were hard. There was so much to read and Rosie just couldn't do it. It was so difficult to get the words to make sense that she could never remember afterwards what they said. She could read things like dates and numbers but that didn't matter when you didn't know the rest of the story.

Rosie walked home past the shops in the main street. She stopped and looked in the antique shop window. There was a funny old watch on a velvet cushion right in the middle.

"It's from Elizabeth the First's time," said a voice beside Rosie. She jumped about a foot in the air, her heart thudding. When she turned round the man who owned the shop was standing in the door looking at her. He was tall, with a thin face and grey hair, but his eyes were very blue.

"It's lovely, isn't it?" he asked, with a little wave towards the watch. "It's more than 400 years old. Imagine who might have owned it. It might even have seen the Spanish Armada."

For a minute Rosie felt as if he could see into her mind. She nodded.

"I'm not very good at history," she said.

"Well, now," said the man, "History is easy. I think you just need to remember that they were people pretty much like us. They lived at a different time, that's all. The things that matter haven't changed. You'll see."

"Can I hold it?" Rosie asked, surprising herself. She hadn't known she meant to ask until the question was out.

The man smiled. "Of course."

Rosie went into the shop. She had never been inside before. It was dark and crammed with odd things. At least 100 watches and clocks ticked away, no one quite in time with the others.

The man opened a door into the window and took out the watch. It was the most beautiful thing Rosie had ever seen. The man placed it in her hand and she was surprised to feel that it was warm, maybe from the sun.

"I wish it could tell us who owned it," she said.

The man smiled.

Rosie was sorry when she had to give the watch back to him and leave the shop to go home.

Rosie could still feel the watch in her hand as she opened the front door and let herself into the house. She felt bad now. When she was at school with Stacey and Jade she could muck around and let on that she didn't care that the teachers and the other pupils thought she was one of the bad kids. When she was on her own it was different and she knew that she really wanted to do well at school. If only she could read!

Rosie's dad was in the kitchen raking in one of the drawers. He already had several things out on the worktop – kitchen scissors, sellotape, a ball of string, the lid of a jam jar and some spare batteries.

"You're late," he said, as soon as Rosie came in the door. "I hope you weren't hanging round the shops with Stacey and Jade again. Your mum is sure the police will bring you home one day."

Rosie thought fast and decided the truth was best. "No, Dad," she said. "The whole class had detention."

Her father glared at her. He was a big man with fair hair that had grown thin at the front. Now there was a frown below the bald patch. "Why?" he asked. "Were you and Stacey mucking around again?"

Rosie didn't want any more trouble. "No," she said. "It was a boy in my class. It wasn't our fault at all. What are you looking for?"

"The superglue," her dad said. He had forgotten about the detention, as Rosie knew he would. "Have you seen it?" he asked. "Gran's broken that vase your mum has on the coffee table."

"Oh, no," said Rosie. "Poor mum. She loves that vase."

"As if I haven't got enough to do tonight!" her father grumped as he slammed the drawer shut. "Amy!" he shouted. "I'll have to fix the vase tomorrow. There's no glue."

Rosie's mother came in from the laundry room with a basket of washing. One look at her face was enough to know that she was in a bad mood too. She slammed the basket down on the table.

"I'll fold those clothes," said Rosie.

"Oh, you will, will you?" said her mum. "A person would almost think you wanted to get in my good books before you tell me why you were late home from school. So, what happened?"

"Detention," Rosie's dad said before she could say anything herself.

"Oh, Rosie," her mum said, "not again." She sat down in a chair and put her head in her hands.

"It wasn't me," Rosie mumbled. "I promise – it wasn't."

"It never is," her mum said, and it was clear from her voice that she meant the exact opposite. "You're such a nice girl, Rosie. Why do you do these silly things at school all the time?"

Rosie grabbed the washing and went out before she started to cry.

Her grandmother was in the sitting room in her big chair in the corner. As always she had her nose in a book.

"Hi, Grandma," Rosie said.

"Hello, Rosie," her grandmother said. "I hear you're in trouble, too."

Rosie liked her grandmother. She didn't ask Rosie questions all the time like her parents. She just chatted away, telling her things about the past or what she had done with her day.

"I'm in bigger trouble than you," said Rosie. "I got detention. But it wasn't my fault."

Her grandmother nodded. "Do you need any help with your homework?" she asked.

Rosie thought her grandmother maybe suspected that she couldn't read. She didn't go on about it, but she was always asking if she could help.

"Not tonight," she said. "I'm too tired."

Rosie folded the washing, ate a sandwich and went to her room. She felt lonely and miserable. Maybe she should have let her grandmother help her with her schoolwork, but now her mum was in the front room too, watching *EastEnders*.

She sat on the floor and took her books out of her bag. As she pulled them out, something fell out on the floor. It was a little red velvet bag, about the right size to fit in the palm of her hand. She opened it and saw the watch from the shop inside.

At first Rosie was scared that she had stolen the watch without even meaning to and that the man in the shop would put the police on her. Then, when she calmed down and thought about it, she realised that he must have put it in the bag himself. But why?

Rosie made up her mind to go back to the shop first thing in the morning. In the meantime she was so scared that something would happen to the watch that she took it to bed with her so it would be safe. She fell asleep with it in her hand. It hadn't been her imagination before – it definitely felt warm.

Chapter 3
The Spanish Are Coming

The next thing Rosie knew, someone had got hold of her arm and was shaking her. She opened her eyes and saw an old woman's face, like her grandmother's, but even more lined.

"Wake up, child! It's me, Kate," the woman said, still holding on to her arm. "There's bad news come and we've got to tell Her Majesty. Come on, up you get!"

Rosie blinked at her as she tried to collect her wits. The bed under her was as hard as the floor, and it felt prickly. She put her hand on it and touched loose straw. Then she looked up and saw she was in a huge kitchen. There were big ovens, an open fireplace with a whole pig in it on a spit, and pots and pans of all shapes and sizes hanging from the rafters. There was no light in the room except the dim glow of a few candles.

"Don't just lie there, child!" Kate said in a cross voice. "Pull yourself together. The news is here and it's bad. The Spanish are coming, and I swear on my mother's grave we'll all be burned for being Protestants, like those poor folk were before."

Rosie's head felt like it would explode. Questions floating around inside her brain and she couldn't think of answers to any of them. They didn't even make sense! Where on earth was she? Where had her house gone? Who was this crazy old woman and what was all this nonsense about burning people?

As Rosie tried to work out what was going on, Kate pulled her to her feet. Some bits of straw still poked out of her clothes. They prickled and she pulled them out. That was when she saw that she was wearing the most awful thing she had ever seen. It was a long brown wool skirt with a long white dress under it and a thing like a tight waistcoat on the top. It smelled like a dog blanket. The Kate woman didn't seem to notice, but then she smelled pretty bad, too, and her apron was covered in black soot.

"Put on your cap, girl," Kate ordered. "And do up your laces. Then go with William here to take this jug of hot ale to Her Majesty. She'll want it before she hears the news. Get a move on."

Rosie tried to tie up the laces on her top before she took the jug and followed the young soldier called William out the door. She had to run to keep up as they went through hall after hall and door after door. Any time they passed other people, she saw from the way they stood huddled close together, eyes watchful, that they were scared.

The only other person who seemed to be in a hurry was a slim, very dark young man with crooked eyebrows. He was speaking in urgent tones to a man in a heavy travelling cloak, whose cape and boots were stained with mud. The traveller had a pointed beard, very black.

As soon as he saw Rosie looking at him his eyes widened with alarm and he stepped back into the shadows.

"Ale for the Queen, eh?" the slim young man with the funny eyebrows said to Rosie. He looked at the jug and took a step forward so that Rosie couldn't see the traveller in the shadows any more. "She'll be waiting for the news," the man said. His voice was not English and he winked at Rosie in a very rude way.

Rosie blushed and hurried after William, who was waiting for her to catch up. Finally they came to a door where a soldier with a sword stood guard. William knocked, and at a word from inside, the guard opened the door and stood back to let Rosie go in.

Rosie found it hard to breathe, and there was a lump in her throat so big she could barely swallow. The room was large and so was everything in it. The bed was huge, with curtains all round it and more fabric draped on top. There were seven or eight candles burning, all set in silver candle-sticks. The walls were covered in beautiful hangings.

Sitting in front of a mirror was a woman, quite old, with a white face. She was not at all pretty. She had a curved nose and thin, sandy eyebrows and a very big forehead. Her hair was bright ginger, the sort of colour it might have gone if it was really white hair dyed red. She was wearing an amazing dress, tight at the waist with a huge, stiff skirt and a white ruffle around the neck. She was sitting very still, staring at herself in the mirror.

Rosie froze. This was not a dream. She knew for sure that this woman was real, and that she was Queen Elizabeth the First of England. She also knew that it was news of the Spanish Armada that the Queen was going to hear tonight. What was going through her mind as she looked into the glass? Was she afraid?

Just then Rosie looked in the mirror and met the Queen's eyes with their heavy lids. Brilliant, clever eyes, just like in the pictures in Rosie's book.

"Well, are you going to pour it for me, or do I have to get up and do it myself?" the Queen asked.

It was as if Rosie had been slapped. At once she came to life, every nerve tingling. "Yes, Your Majesty – I mean – no!" With hands that shook she picked up the cup on the dressing table and poured the hot ale from the jug into it. She could smell sweet spices and sugar. She filled the cup up to the brim, maybe too near the top. She bit her lip as the Queen lifted it, afraid that it would spill and stain the amazing dress.

Elizabeth didn't spill a drop. She raised the cup to her lips and drank deeply, then put it down again on the table. She looked at herself one more time in the mirror, then put her shoulders back and stood up, turning to face Rosie. She was not as tall as Rosie, by several inches, but there was a strength in her, a force of will that made her seem bigger. The candle-light blazed on the jewels that were around her neck, on her fingers, and stitched onto the fabric of her clothes.

Rosie was too stunned to be afraid. She could see that the Queen was breathing fast. There was a tiny muscle flickering under the white skin on her forehead. There were tired lines around the corners of her eyes. The hands resting on the fabulous, stiff skirts were thin, a little swollen at the knuckles. Rosie wondered if they hurt her, like her own grandmother's did sometimes.

Rosie looked up and met the Queen's eye by accident. She turned away fast but the Queen stared at her with faint amusement.

"What are you afraid of?" she asked. "I won't let the Spanish burn you." Her smile was self-mocking, as though she knew that she was weak in some ways, as well as strong in others. "I may well need you myself one day."

Rosie couldn't believe what she had just heard. "Need me?" she said in amazement. "But you're the wisest queen in the world. I can hardly even read."

The Queen looked surprised. "Some of my ladies-in-waiting cannot read at all," she said. "Perhaps I should make one of them a maid and you a lady. Do you think you would like to spend all day here, waiting to pick up my handkerchief if I dropped it? I cannot bend over far enough in this stiff dress to do even that for myself."

"I couldn't imagine wearing a dress like that," said Rosie, before she knew she was speaking. "This one is bad enough."

The Queen looked shocked for a minute, then she laughed. "You are an odd child. This dress cost more than you will earn in your lifetime. Would you really not like to wear it?"

"Not on your life," said Rosie.

The Queen laughed again. "Well, this has been most interesting. But off you go, now, child, before you insult my belongings any more."

Rosie picked up the cup. "Thank you, Your Majesty."

Chapter 4
Fear

Back in the kitchen Kate eyed Rosie closely. "You were away a long time. What kept you?" she asked.

Rosie was lost for words. This was far worse than at school. She had no idea what she was doing here in the past, and no clue why she had woken up there. The weirdest thing about it all was that the longer she was here, the more she forgot about being anywhere else.

"Well, don't just stand there, girl," Kate said, fed up with waiting. "No one's going to sleep tonight. Go and get more firewood, and we'll at least keep warm. There'll be food needed, and hot ale. God knows what'll happen to us all. But I know what'll happen to you, if you don't look sharp, because I'll do it myself!"

"Yes, Kate," Rosie said. "Of course I will." She hurried out towards the door beyond the ovens and the racks of vegetables and strings of onions.

Rosie worked on and off for what seemed like hours. She lost all sense of time until she saw the light on the stone floor and knew the sky was pale blue outside. From the little bits of trees she could see, it was high summer. Full green leaves flickered in a sharp wind.

Rosie could just hear snatches of talk as other servants met and spoke for a moment here and there. There was fear everywhere, and people whispered about war and about fighting in the streets. Everyone said that they were willing to die rather than give in to the enemy.

"I've heard about the Spanish," a kitchen-maid said with a shudder. "They'll be all over the place, killing people for no reason, burning houses, barns, anything. Give them a sideways look and they'll have you."

"Come on!" said one of the grooms crossly. "You're scaring people. Why should they do that?"

The maid swung round to face him. "Because that's what they do when they win a war, like they're doing in the Netherlands right now. I tell you, if they come here they'll be in our streets and our houses forever."

No one argued with her any more. It looked like they had all heard stories about the Netherlands and they knew what she said was true.

There was a footman called Harry and he stopped by Rosie while he grabbed a couple of slices of bread and a little meat.

"Are you scared?" Harry asked her with a grin. He was a big fellow, about twenty or so, not very tall.

Should Rosie lie? *That would be stupid*, she thought. *If you had any brains at all you ought to be scared.* "Yes," she said, staring Harry in the eye. "I am scared. Why do the Spanish want to invade us, anyway?"

"Are you a fool, girl?" Harry asked, amazed.

"That means you don't know," Rosie answered, taking another bite of meat.

"Of course I know!" Harry said. "Mainly I expect it's because of the Church, and Bloody Mary. Also our sailors go all over the New World and rob their ships of gold and stuff, and that doesn't help." Harry grinned even more widely.

"Who's Mary," asked Rosie, "and why did you call her Bloody?"

"Everyone does, stupid! Has no one ever told you anything at all?" Harry's voice rose as if he couldn't believe that Rosie knew so little.

"Are you going to tell me or not?" Rosie snapped.

"Mary was the Queen's half-sister," Harry replied at once. "The daughter of old King Henry's first wife, who was Spanish, and Catholic of course, because everyone was

Catholic then. When Mary became queen she married the King of Spain and wanted to make us all Catholic again, and she burned all the important people who'd changed to being Protestant, and lots of others too. That's why people call her Bloody Mary. Because of all the blood she spilled."

"She burned them?" A horrible picture came into Rosie's mind of someone standing on a pile of wood, and the smoke and flames roaring up around them. She couldn't even think how much it would hurt. She had only ever burned her hand once, but she could still remember how bad the pain was.

Harry's grin faded for a moment. "Yes. My grandad was one of them. My ma says so, but she won't talk about it."

"I'm sorry," Rosie said quickly. She really meant it. She couldn't even think of how awful that would be.

Harry shrugged. "I don't know how you don't know that. Where the devil have you been living all your life?"

Rosie couldn't answer that, so she changed the subject. "Did we really steal a lot of gold from the Spanish?" she asked.

"Yes," said Harry. "All over the Americas, and the West Indies, everywhere we could. We call it being buccaneers – that's sort of a polite word for pirates." He shrugged his shoulders and then went on. "But the Queen pretends she doesn't know anything about it, and thinks they're all heroes."

"All the buccaneers?" Rosie asked.

"Yeah, of course," Harry said. "I'd like to go to sea one day, with Francis Drake."

"So would I," Rosie said at once.

Harry laughed. "A girl at sea?" he said. "Now, that would be a sight to behold. It's bad luck for a ship to have women on it. You're some girl, Rosie, you really are."

Chapter 5
Kings and Queens

The long day passed, doing one job after another. Rosie was glad to be busy because it helped her forget about being afraid. No one knew exactly what the messengers had said to the Queen, but she had left for the seaport of Tilbury, where most of the British ships were in harbour ready to sail against the Armada.

By dusk Rosie was so tired she felt as if she could have gone to sleep standing up. Her eyes stung and her back and feet ached.

"Have you eaten?" Kate asked Rosie in a sharp voice, stopping in front of her where she stood with a basket of vegetables in her hands. The basket was heavy and Rosie was so tired she was afraid she was going to drop it.

"Put it down, girl, before you fall over," Kate told her. "No one can say you're lazy, that's for sure. Sit down over here." She pointed to a wooden stool by the long oak table. "I'll get you some stew. Then you can go to bed."

Rosie thanked her, put the vegetables in the rack, then sat down to wait for the food. She was hungry enough to have eaten anything.

Actually it was really good, even though it was served on a chunk of bread for a plate, and there was a mug of ale to go with it. Kate served herself some as well, and sat opposite Rosie in the wavering candle-light. It was warm and cosy, and for a little while Rosie forgot to be afraid.

"Don't let that daft Harry upset you," Kate said after a while. "He's just scared and trying to make you feel worse than he does."

"He was OK," Rosie replied, brushing it off as if the stories of burning people were not that bad. She paused. Should she ask Kate about it?

"He just said a bit about the Queen's sister," Rosie said after a second, "who was born before we all became Protestants ..." She stopped because she did not want to sound stupid, or for Kate to be angry with her.

Kate snorted. "Ha! Bloody Mary. That's what we called her, and it was a good name for her, too."

"And she did everything she did because of the King of Spain that she was married to?" Rosie asked.

"In a way. You know we all became Protestants under King Henry, when he stood up to the Pope in Rome and set up a whole new church. Then we were allowed to read the Bible in our own language. And pray to God ourselves instead of giving all our money to priests and bishops so they could do it for us. But Mary stuck to the Catholic faith, and when she became queen, she wanted to go back. She was willing to torture and burn any of us who had turned to the new church." Kate shivered, and her faced paled and became tight with fear.

"I can still hear the screams in my mind, and smell smoke, and flesh burning," she said. "They were terrible times, Rosie. We don't want them back. I'd sooner be in my grave than see that again."

"But Mary's dead, isn't she?" Rosie asked.

"To be sure, poor soul," Kate agreed. "But her husband, King Philip of Spain, isn't."

"Why are you sorry for her?" Rosie asked, puzzled by the pity she had heard in Kate's voice. "You just said how she spilled all that blood."

"She didn't live a happy life," Kate told her. "Don't you know the story? King Henry put her mother away, and said that Mary wasn't his lawful child. That was a lie. He was angry because her mother had given him only one daughter. All their sons died. And then he fell madly in love with Anne Boleyn, our queen's mother."

A memory stirred in Rosie's mind, but she couldn't grasp hold of it. It was something sad and ugly.

Kate's face was grim. "And of course Anne gave him only the one daughter too, our Queen Elizabeth as she is now. So he grew tired of Anne too, and people gossiped about her with all sorts of stories that she was a witch, and other nonsense." She stopped, her voice choked with sadness.

Rosie wanted to ask what had happened to Anne, but she couldn't think of any words that would not make Kate feel worse.

"They cut her head off," Kate said softly. "She was a foolish girl, but she didn't deserve that. Elizabeth was only a child then, but life wasn't easy for her either, poor soul. She was a prisoner of one sort or another, most of her youth."

"But when the King died, then Elizabeth became queen?" Rosie asked.

"Lord help us, no!" Kate said. She rolled her eyes. "Girl, you know so little! Where were you brought up? After Anne Boleyn was dead

Jane Seymour was queen, and she gave King Henry a son at last. Poor, ill child, he was, and so was Queen Jane, poor thing."

"So the son was king after Henry?" Rosie asked, hoping she was right this time.

"Yes, King Edward VI. But he died when he was still a child. Then Bloody Mary, as the elder daughter, was queen next. And she couldn't have children at all, which wasn't so amazing, since her husband was King of Spain, and they hardly ever slept under the same roof!"

"And now we have Queen Elizabeth!" Rosie said, sounding pleased.

"God bless her!" Kate added with deep feeling.

"But who'll come after her?" Rosie asked.

Kate's cheeks went red all of a sudden and her eyes filled with tears. She reached out and hit Rosie hard on the side of the head, making her ears sting. Rosie was so startled she didn't say anything at all. She sat quite still, blinking. Then as she stared at Kate she saw that for all her brave words and busy hands with the kitchen jobs, she too was afraid, not just a little bit, but so deep inside it made her legs shake and her stomach sick, just like Rosie's.

Rosie wanted to say something that would make Kate feel better, but what was there? If Edward VI was dead, and Mary was dead and no one had any children, who would be left when Elizabeth died? Would it be King Philip of Spain? And would he burn everyone who was Protestant? Was that what really scared Kate?

"We'll just have to beat him," Rosie said in as strong a voice as she could manage. Even so, it wobbled a bit. "We'll fight him forever, if we have to."

"Fight who?" Kate said. "What are you talking about?"

"The King of Spain," Rosie answered. "We'll have to beat him and his Armada."

"Lord help you, of course we will!" said Kate. "He won't ever be King of England, that's for certain. Is that what you're scared of? You've forgotten, but there was Mary Queen of

Scots, may God forgive her for her sins. Her son's alive and well, and they'll bring him up Protestant, you can sleep easy on that. There's nobody more Protestant than the Scots lords – as Mary found out, the stupid creature."

Now Rosie was really confused. Yet another Queen Mary! A different one.

Kate shook her head. "Did no one ever teach you a thing when you were growing up? Well, you must know they cut her head off, because that was only last year. Queen of all Scotland, she was, until she married one too many bad husbands, and the Scots lords threw her out of the country. She came here to take refuge in England, thinking we'd keep her safe, but she had ideas about being Queen of England and sending us all back to being Catholic again. Like I said, may God forgive her. She plotted against our queen so many times Elizabeth had to get rid of her." Kate shook her head. "Went very hard with the Queen, that did," she said, "seeing as Mary was royal too. But Mary left her no choice."

"So they cut her head off too, Mary Queen of Scots?" Rosie thought of Anne Boleyn, the

Queen's mother, and now this. No wonder Elizabeth found it hard to be queen. It was more dangerous than Rosie would ever have thought.

"Why would they let that Mary's son be King of England?" she said aloud.

"There's no one else," Kate replied sadly. "Mary had the same great grandfather as the Queen."

"So she and Elizabeth were sort of cousins?"

"That's right."

Rosie went to bed still thinking about all the love and hate, all the high hopes and fear and fighting. No wonder Elizabeth looked tired and lonely. But Elizabeth couldn't afford to let anyone guess that she might be afraid too.

Chapter 6
Traitor!

The next day was far worse. Rosie was going down a dark passage when she heard two men talking. One was a footman, the other a stable boy. At first everything they said seemed to be just chatter about coming and going, horses, carriages, distances. Rosie was about to go around them when she understood that they were talking about the Queen leaving for Tilbury. Then one of them said that 'Diego' had gone with her. That was the dark young man Rosie had seen in the passage the night the news arrived, talking to the stranger with the muddy boots – surely one of the messengers from Spain!

"He went with the Queen?" Rosie broke in. "You're sure?"

"Diego?" one of the men asked. "Of course."

"But he's Spanish!" Rosie protested. "He could kill her!"

One of the men put his hands on his hips and stared at Rosie as if she were mad. "Why would he do that? We'd kill him, and it wouldn't change anything. We'd still beat the Armada and he'd have died for nothing. Believe me, Diego's much too fond of life for that."

But Rosie knew she was right – and that something was very wrong. She remembered the way the man with muddy boots had slunk off into the shadows. She knew guilt when she saw it. There was no point in arguing with the men – she must do something herself. If anyone killed the Queen, they would all be living in a different world. How could they be so stupid as not to know that?

The Queen had gone to Tilbury. Everyone would know where to find her there. Rosie turned around and went back the way she had come, then out of the side door and around to the stables. It was dark, and if anyone saw her they took no notice. They thought she was just one of the maids sent to do something for someone. Thank goodness that in the dim light they could not see how she was shaking. Nor could they know that her heart was beating so hard that it felt as if it were trying to break out of her chest.

Rosie knew what she had to do. She had never ridden a horse on her own before, and she had no real idea where this palace she had found herself in was. But somehow she must take a horse and find her way to the port of Tilbury to warn the Queen.

She was in the stable now. There were all sorts of horses, some for carriages, some for riding. How was she ever going to pick the right one, and get a bridle on it, and a saddle? Close to, in the smell of hay and straw and live animals, all the horses seemed enormous! She could hear them stamp their feet and blow through their nostrils. They knew there was a stranger in the stable. Were horses dangerous? What if one kicked her, or trod on her? Did they bite?

But then Rosie remembered that Diego had gone with the Queen! England's fate might depend on Rosie's warning her in time. Rosie thought about the Queen's face in the mirror, how tired and alone she had looked, just for a moment, and how kind she had been to Rosie.

Rosie chose a quiet horse who bent her head down so Rosie could reach her. Rosie had been horse-riding a few times and she knew where the saddle and bridle went but it was hard to put them on without help. Finally she managed. She pulled the strap of the saddle as tight as she could round the horse's belly. It would be stupid if it all slipped off and landed her in the dirt.

Then Rosie opened the stable door and led the horse out into the yard. It was not hard to get up onto her back without help as she was a small horse and she did what Rosie asked without any fuss when Rosie slapped her back to make her ride off. No one tried to stop her – no one seemed to be on guard in the same way now that the Queen was not here any more.

Rosie just kept going until she was out of sight of the huge palace where they had been staying. Then she began to think how she would get to Tilbury. What direction was it? On the sea, of course, and that had to be south. But which was south? She had no idea. How stupid was this?

The wind was a little gusty and there were clouds in the sky so Rosie could see only some of the stars. There was a weather-cock on the roof of one of the bigger houses nearby. The wind swung it round, first one way and then the other, but the signs for north, south, east and west stayed still. And there was a road leading south – that was the way to go.

Rosie kicked the horse and it broke into a trot, then a canter. She was thrown all around and had to cling on or she would have been on the ground, probably with broken bones, and no use to anyone.

Rosie seemed to ride for miles before there were more cross-roads. There was a sign where the roads met. She stopped as close to the sign as she could and stared at it. The writing was black, burned into the wood with something hot, and the letters were crooked. Was that a B or a P? The word might be 'Tilbury'. The other direction was two words, so that had to be wrong. She stared at the first one again, trying to make herself remember the shape of it so she would know it next time. Why was she so stupid?

Rosie urged the horse to a canter again. It was hard to hang on, and the saddle was like a rock. Her backside felt like it was bruised black and blue, her legs throbbed and her hands were scraped to blisters by the reins.

She came to another sign which she could hardly even see in the dark. This time she traced the letters with her fingers. Only one of them had a T at the beginning, and it seemed about the right length. She felt it again, but it wasn't going to tell her anything more. She went that way.

Chapter 7

A Rest

By sunrise Rosie had stopped on the brow of a hill from where she could see light on water far ahead. She had to be within a few miles of the coast. But was it Tilbury?

The early morning wind was chill off the sea and Rosie realised with a shock that she was not only very, very tired, but also hungry and cold. Then she thought with shame that the horse must be hungry too, maybe even more than she was. After all, she had not only come all this way, she had carried Rosie. She slid off, and led the horse towards an inn with a sign painted with a golden lion, swinging in the wind.

Rosie had no money. She only thought of that now. The last thing she wanted to do was beg, but she had no choice, for the horse at least. The poor animal deserved better than she had given her so far.

She led the horse into the stony yard and looked around. There was a butt of water, and the horse saw it before Rosie did! She pulled a little to get to the water faster, and was just about to put her nose into it when a man came out of the back door, a cloth in his hand. He was tall and thin. He had grey hair, but his eyes were clear blue and as mild as the summer sky.

"Don't let her drink yet," he told Rosie. "Walk her back and forth a bit first to let her cool down. Take the saddle off and rub her with this." He held out the cloth. "There's hay in the stable over there you can give her. Then let her drink. Cold water on a hot stomach's bad for a horse. You wouldn't want to do that to her."

Rosie took the cloth, and felt her face burn for not knowing how to care for the horse. The man must think she was an idiot, and a cruel idiot as well. "Thank you," she muttered, and her eyes stung with sudden tears of shame. She walked with her head down, pulling the horse with her, away from the water.

In the stable she did as the man had told her, rubbing the horse gently, most of all where she was wet with sweat. She pulled down hay for her, but did not stop the rubbing while she ate, talking to her all the time.

Rosie felt a little silly when she saw that the man was standing in the doorway. She turned to face him and found he was smiling. He had a plate in one hand with bread and meat on it, and a large mug of ale in the other.

Rosie stopped rubbing the horse and the horse pushed her nose into the middle of her back, quite hard, knocking her off balance. She stumbled forward, tripped over an uneven stone and landed on her hands and knees in the straw.

The man laughed, but it was a happy sound. He was not mocking Rosie. "Your horse likes you," he said with a smile. "She wants your complete attention." He set the plate and the mug down on top of a table and held out his hand to pull Rosie to her feet. His mild blue eyes looked at her seriously. "You've come a long way at some speed. You must need to do something important."

Rosie met the man's gaze and had a strange, happy feeling that she had seen him somewhere before and it had been good. His blue eyes seemed to see right into Rosie's heart. Her fear slipped away. She even felt less tired. Who was this good, kind man?

"You'll get there faster in the end if you give the mare a rest for a while, let her get her energy back," the man said. "She's a good animal. And while she's sleeping a bit, you should do the same. You'll need your wits sharp when you get there. Eat your food." The man nodded towards the plate and the mug. "Then go to sleep in the loft. There's plenty of hay up there to keep you warm. I'll come for you in an hour or two. Go towards the sea for a mile, then, where the road forks, take the right turn and it'll lead you all the way to Tilbury."

47

"Thank you." Rosie was so grateful that she forgot to ask how the man knew where she was going. She no longer felt ashamed that she had no money to pay for the food. She knew it did not matter.

The man smiled at her and there was a peace inside him that for a moment made his face glow. Then he turned and went out again, crossing the cobbled yard back to the kitchen door.

Chapter 8
Tilbury

It was a bright, windy morning just before noon when Rosie at last rode into Tilbury and saw the harbour full of ships. Most of them had wide, round sides and guns showing at every opening. They looked tiny on the rough blue water. It would be a brave, risky adventure to go out of sight of land in them, let alone around the world.

But Rosie had no time to worry about that now. The wind was rising, as if for a summer storm, and the Armada was on its way. The streets were crowded with men, most of them sailors getting ready to go to sea to fight their more powerful enemy. Some would never come back. Would they be injured, or lose arms or legs, or be taken prisoner, or go down to the bottom of the sea with their ships? They might be burned. There was nowhere to escape to from a ship on fire.

Rosie must find the Queen. She stopped a man and asked him where she was. "I'm a royal messenger and I have something for her," she added. Of course this wasn't true, but it wasn't a complete lie either.

The man looked as if he did not believe her, then he looked more carefully at the fine quality of the horse and its saddle, and told her where to go. Rosie rode on as the man had told her until she came to a huge house high above the harbour. There she was stopped at the door by soldiers armed with muskets and big lances with curved ends. A blow with one of those would have torn a man's insides to pieces.

Rosie got off her horse and spoke in a polite manner. "I'm a servant to the Queen and I have an important message for Her

Majesty," she said as firmly as she could, but she heard her voice wobble.

"Of course you do," one of the soldiers said in a voice that made it clear he didn't believe her. "Who says so?" he asked. "You?"

"Of course, me," Rosie told him. "Who else is there?" The moment the words were out of her mouth she knew they were a mistake. "I'm sorry I was rude!" she said quickly. "But it's very important. The Queen's in danger, and she needs to know."

"We're all in danger, girl," the second soldier told her. "The Spanish are coming, haven't you heard?"

"One of them is already here!" Rosie said. "Please listen to me! I have to tell the Queen! He's a spy – she doesn't know."

"And you do? My, my! Well, you tell me, and I'll see that she gets to hear," the first soldier said, and laughed.

Rosie could see that they didn't believe her one bit, and she couldn't blame them. But if she didn't tell the Queen about Diego, then

Diego might kill her, and Rosie couldn't bear the thought of that.

"Do you want to be the one who gets blamed if a spy kills the Queen?" she asked. "It'll be your fault, because you could have stopped it, but you didn't." For a moment she thought about Laura Webb, and how she always went along with it when the others picked on her. Rosie wasn't going to give in like that. She took a step closer to the solider. "Or maybe you want her killed!" she said. "Are you a Spanish spy too?"

Now the soldier was really angry. His fair skin flushed red and his hands gripped his lance so hard that the bones in his knuckles were white. "You say that again," he said, "and I'll give you a swipe with this that just might take your head off!"

Seeing his rage, and his fear too, Rosie thought he might just do that. "I know you aren't a spy," she said, and tried to gulp back her own fear. "But you need to show how loyal you are to the Queen by doing the right thing now. Because one of the servants in there is a spy."

Then Rosie had an idea. She took a very deep breath. She was trying to stop herself from shaking. Her throat was so tight she couldn't speak. "Go in there and tell the Queen that the girl who brings her hot ale has come to pick up her handkerchief, and to warn her of danger. Just do that!"

The soldier blinked. "If she has me thrown out as a fool," he said, "I'll find you and box your ears until you can't hear for a week, do you understand?"

"Yes," Rosie said. "Now just go and tell her!"

While he went into the house, Rosie was shown into a waiting room outside the Queen's chamber. She stood stiff and grubby among the elegant royal servants and advisers. They all wore short, wide breeches and long stockings. At any other time she might have thought they looked funny, but now it was all deadly serious. Some of them were old men, with silver hair and grave faces. They talked in low voices. Rosie could see they were afraid. It was plain in the way they stood, in their restless little movements, in their stiff hands and the way they pulled at their jackets for no reason.

Rosie learned that there had been a big sea battle at a place called Gravelines, off the coast of the Netherlands. She felt sick as she heard the news. Many sailors had died and they had used almost all the cannon-balls the navy had. How could England possibly defend herself with so much already lost? All along the coast the beacon fires were built, huge piles of dry timber waiting to be lit as a warning to people inland that the enemy had landed. There would be fighting, and perhaps they would all be killed.

Then at last, when the Royal advisers had all gone, Rosie was shown in.

Chapter 9
The Queen

The Queen was standing in the room alone. The sunlight streamed through the diamond-shaped panes of the windows and made patterns on the floor. The Queen's jewels dazzled Rosie's eyes, catching sparks like bright flames, yet the Queen herself looked oddly small.

"Well, girl who picks up my handkerchiefs and insults my clothes," the Queen said, "what is it you have to warn me about?" She looked pale and her voice was tired and rather rough, as if she had been up for too many nights, for too many years, and in the end, always found herself alone.

"Your Majesty, the night the messenger came about the Armada, I saw that man Diego talking in the corridor to a man in a cloak and muddy boots who had come from some other land. The man hid as soon as he saw me, and Diego stepped between us to stop me from seeing where he went. When I heard that Diego had come with you, I was afraid he might harm you." Now that she said it, it sounded foolish. It could have meant anything, or nothing. The Queen must think she was an idiot.

The Queen turned away, as if to hide her face from Rosie. "I know that Diego is a spy, but I thank you for coming to tell me."

Rosie did not know what to say. She felt really silly now. The Queen had known all along. How stupid was that?

The Queen turned back to her and there were bright tears on her cheek. "I wish that all my subjects were as loyal as you are, child. What is your name?"

"Rosie – Your Majesty," Rosie said, feeling happiness rise up inside her like the heat of the sun. "I was so afraid he'd hurt you."

"It will take more than one traitor to hurt me, Rosie," the Queen said. "I've seen many come and go."

Rosie remembered the stories Kate had told her, of the men who had wanted Queen Elizabeth to be their wife, and how she had loved some of them but always refused to marry. To do that would have been to hand over her power to one who might use it less wisely. Elizabeth never forgot how Mary Queen of Scots had lost everything because of men. How much had Elizabeth given up to serve England? Perhaps no one even guessed.

The Queen spoke across Rosie's thoughts, having got over her moment of emotion.

"You came all this way alone?" she asked.

"Yes, Your Majesty," Rosie said.

"Really?" the Queen looked surprised. "And how did you find a horse to carry you?"

"I ... took one of yours," Rosie said. "I didn't think you'd mind. At least – I hoped not."

The Queen was smiling now. "I imagine you are hungry?" she asked. "All of a sudden I am too. I am tired of admirals and lords and advisers. Fetch me some chicken from the kitchen, Rosie, and some syllabub, and a little wine. And bring enough for two. Do you like syllabub?"

Rosie had no idea, but she decided she would eat it even if it turned out be made of frogs' legs. "Yes, Your Majesty," she said.

"Good," said Queen Elizabeth. "Bring plenty."

The next day Rosie stood in the crowd at the docks as the Queen spoke to the hundreds of people that filled every possible space. Sailors were packed in among tradesmen, clerks, shopkeepers, and the craftsmen and workers who built and fitted the ships of the navy.

The Queen said a lot of things about being brave, about fighting, and about loyalty. Rosie heard it all, but one thing she never forgot. "I have the weak body of a woman," the Queen said, "but I have the heart and stomach of a king – and a King of England, at that."

Rosie cheered with all the others, shouting until her throat hurt. She felt a fierce joy within her, a real pride in being part of her country's history. Even though she already knew that they would win, she knew the moment that the whole crowd started to believe it too, whatever the odds against them. And she knew that they had decided that even if they lost at sea, if the Spanish landed, then they would all fight until every last man and woman was dead. They would never give in. If the Queen could defy Spain, then so could they.

The Queen was afraid, Rosie knew that. She had seen it in her weary face, the stiff, old woman's hands, the tears on her cheeks. She had laughed over the dinner they had shared, and the sticky sweet syllabub, which was actually pretty good. But Rosie knew that standing up to Spain had cost her almost all that she had. The short time with a serving girl who expected nothing of her, and would ride all night to warn her of a danger she already knew all about, was a chance, just for an hour or so, to not have to be the Queen at all.

Chapter 10
The Storm

Then came the waiting. The weather grew worse, the terrible gale became stronger. It was one of the worst storms anyone could remember. The wind screamed round the low walls of the houses and the heavy straw thatch of the roofs was soaked with rain. Branches of trees were blown off. Down by the shore the waves crashed home with terrible force. Each wave crashed into the wall at the dock-side and sent white spray into the air. Anyone so foolish as to get too close was likely to be swept away.

It went on for days while everyone huddled together inside their houses and halls, waiting for news. Rosie stayed in the big house where the Queen was. The Queen gave orders that Rosie should be fed and given a place to sleep. Sometimes Rosie took her food or drink, but she never saw her alone again.

The Queen was pale. She paced the floor back and forth. She spoke with her advisers, but their faces were white and strained also. Would the Spanish invade, as soon as the storm had spent itself? The beacon fires were sodden. How could they warn people now? Inland, they would all be taken by surprise. They would hear noise in the streets and look up from their work to see Spanish soldiers!

Then came the news. It was just a shout at first, a messenger panting hard, covered in dust and sweat, his hair wild. "They're sunk! The whole Armada of Spain has been driven north by the wind and wrecked up around the coast of Scotland, and even Ireland. There's never been a storm like it. The sea has beaten them for us!"

At first there was silence, a moment of awe. To be saved was such a wonderful surprise that, for a moment, they could not grasp what had happened. Then the cheer began, the sound growing and swelling until it filled the air and spread through every man and woman who had waited in terror.

Rosie looked across at where the Queen stood, with her advisers all around her. They were dizzy with relief, and cheering, laughing, praising her, giving thanks. But who would they have blamed had the sea not saved them?

For a moment the Queen looked at Rosie and she smiled at her. She took out her handkerchief, and dropped it. Then she walked away, her advisers following her.

Rosie went over and picked up the handkerchief. There was something under it – a small velvet bag. As soon as Rosie picked it up and felt how warm it was, she knew it was the watch. It had been meant for her all along.

Rosie walked away with a new glow inside her. She had never felt so grateful. And then, as she felt the wind on her skin, she thought of the terror and power of the sea. It had saved

England, but it had drowned so many people. She could not be quite happy because there was sadness for them too, and the families they would never see again. She shut her eyes against the glare of the light.

Chapter 11
Speaking Out

Rosie opened her eyes and blinked, confused. An alarm bell was ringing and for a wild second she had no idea where she was. Then she realised it was the clock on her own chest of drawers, in her own bedroom at home. It was time to get up and go to school.

She wanted so much to cling onto her dream of Queen Elizabeth's time. She felt as if all the strong and beautiful things she had learned were slipping out of her grasp and leaving nothing behind. She was just Rosie Sands again, who wasn't really stupid but had to hang out with the stupid kids to hide the fact she couldn't read very well. There was no queen to be her friend, no one at all who believed in her. The watch belonged to a different Rosie, and she would have to take it back to the shop today.

At school, Mr Jones was in a bad mood again even though the clever kids knew the answers to his questions about facts and figures. Laura Webb gave an amazing talk – of course – about how Queen Elizabeth defeated the Armada. At the end she looked at the class through her glasses and gave a big, geeky smile.

"Like Queen Elizabeth had anything to do with it, swot," Kris Cole said with a sneer. "She was only a woman. It was the sailors that won it for us, and the storm. We just got lucky. For once the weather worked for us. Not like at the football on Saturday."

"Elizabeth was a great queen," Laura said, her nose going red.

"Yeah?" Kris laughed. "You just think that because you're a girl. Name one thing she did that wasn't a total fluke."

Rosie was angry now, too. She shot to her feet. "Elizabeth *was* a great queen!" she said loudly. "She stopped the Protestants and Catholics burning each other the way they did under the kings and queens before her."

The class went quiet. Stacey turned round very slowly. Her mouth was hanging open so far with surprise that Rosie could see the chewing gum inside. Beside her, Jade's eyes were nearly popping out of her head in shock.

For a minute Rosie thought about shutting up and sitting down again but then she remembered Elizabeth and how brave she had been. She wouldn't have pretended to be stupid just so stupid people wouldn't bully her. Not on your life.

Rosie took a deep breath and spoke again. "Queen Elizabeth was wise and brave and she thought about the country more than herself," she said. "She never got married so she could keep the power to do the right things for England in her own hands. We got rich and great because we stopped fighting wars, because Elizabeth was clever enough to avoid them. Because we weren't off fighting we had time to make really good buildings and schools … and industry and stuff. And there were great poets and writers, too, like Shakespeare. All over the world they know about him, don't they?"

Laura Webb nodded. Rosie risked a look at Zack Edwards. He was smiling.

"When they thought the Armada was going to attack," she went on, "everyone was scared stiff, and so was Elizabeth. She wasn't stupid, she knew the danger, but she pretended she was sure they would win. She went and spoke to all the people on Tilbury dockside, out in the wind, and it was beginning to rain, but she never stopped. She made us all believe that we'd never be beaten, even if we had to fight in the streets or the forests or the marshes."

Laura gave Rosie a thumbs-up. Rosie smiled back and took a deep breath before she went on. "It isn't big weapons or lots of soldiers that win battles," she said, "it's being brave, and never giving in. And if you don't know that then you don't know anything about real history."

There was a moment's silence. Rosie sat down, her legs shaking.

"Good heavens!" Mr Jones said, his eyes wide with surprise. "Well said, Rosie. You see? I knew you had it in you."

Rosie said nothing. She was just as surprised as Mr Jones. It felt almost like being at Tilbury again, with the Queen smiling at her and dropping her handkerchief to let her know she'd seen her. She was glad she had told the class the truth about Elizabeth. And she was glad that she had shown Jade and Stacey the truth about herself.

Suddenly she felt the watch burn warm in her pocket. Elizabeth was proud of her, too.